To my lovely family.
Thank you for all your support over the years.

Violet Clough

THE BOY WHO HAD NOTHING

AUSTIN MACAULEY PUBLISHERS™

LONDON • CAMBRIDGE • NEW YORK • SHARJAH

A CIP catalogue record for this title is available from the British Library.

ISBN 9781035870622 (Paperback)
ISBN 9781035870639 (ePub e-book)

www.austinmacauley.com

First Published 2024
Austin Macauley Publishers Ltd®
1 Canada Square
Canary Wharf
London
E14 5AA

Nanna and Grandad Jones – a librarian and baker.

Nanna and Grandad Smith – own a small farm with pigs, sheep and cows.

Mum – Mary Jones (newsagents shop worker).

Dad – David Smith (carpenter).

Tim Smith – born 25th Dec, 1993.

Mary & David met when David, bought a newspaper in Mary's shop.

Sister Sally Johnson Harper: 28 when met up with Tim – three girls and husband John.

Brother Paul Johnson: 26 when met up with Tim – two boys with wife Louise.

Biological parents Kate and Paul Johnson – both deceased due to car accident.

Tim's girlfriend Jennifer – her parents, Bob and Julia; brother, Jake; and friend, Emma.

Synopsis

Mary and David are strict parents to their only child, Tim. Coincidently, Mary & David are also from single-child families. Tim is bullied as a schoolchild because he has a stammer and wears glasses. Tim finds out as a teenager he is adopted which rocks his world but opens the door to a new life for him.

Child

When Tim had been born eight weeks earlier, he was only 8 lbs in weight. A beautiful smiley bouncy baby boy, everyone wanted to cuddle Tim. He had a lot of wavy fine hair and always smelt nice; his clothes were knitted outfits made by his mother. Mary was strict though, and would only allow the baby to be picked up if he was needing a feed or nappy change. This way she found he could watch her go about the household chores without wanting to be held. She would sing as she tidied up the house, with Tim watching from his rocking baby chair that his dad had made.

David would look at his son with such happiness he thought he would burst. His son was all he wished for in life. A loving wife and a baby. He was content. Mary and David would coo over Tim without spoiling him. They had worked so hard and had years of pain trying for a baby. It was equivalent to winning the lottery for them both. When nanna and grandad visited on both sides of the family (which was regular), their lives seemed complete. Mary would bath Tim, dress him in her knitted outfits and stare at this gorgeous gift in front of her. To say she was besotted was an understatement. She kept a diary, she wrote in it every day, all of little Tim's sleeping habits, how much milk he would take from his bottle, walks they went on, and how much he weighed. He was putting on a few pounds now that he drank all his milk feed.

She especially loved going out to the shops with her lovely pram; it was a silver cross style and she bought it for £50 from the second-hand shop in town and it looked brand new. She made the bedding for it from old sheets she had in her airing cupboard and crocheted two blankets. She felt proud of her work.

As Tim got older, he was able to sit up on the walks as the section behind where he sat reclined up and down. They would go to the park and take in the fresh air, enjoy the smell of the grass and the prettiness of the daisies and buttercups growing in the clover. Mary would buy ice cream and find a seat to sit on. She would always push her finger into the top of the cornet to give Tim a taste.

At home, Mary and David always cooked from scratch. They never threw anything away, and everything went into something. It was at this point Mary started to push her home cooked dinners through a sieve so that Tim could have a small meal at 6 pm. He would be in his high chair while Mum and Dad were sitting at the table. Mum would have a mouthful of her meal, put her knife and fork down and pick up a small teaspoon and give Tim a taste. He pulled a few faces now and then at the different flavours but always ate what he was given.

In the evening when Tim was asleep in his cot, Mary and David would sit watching TV or would listen to the radio. They never went out; they were ecstatic, just the three of them in their happy place.

Mary would boil the kettle and make tea for them both and listen to the sound of silence, and they would reflect on their journey to have a baby. David would give his wife a cuddle and tell her how great she was at being a mother. He would look at his wife and proudly tell her how perfect his life is; they had a small amount of money but were not millionaires in terms of richness.

David picked up a photograph encased in a shiny silver frame of all three of them from the mantelpiece and he turned to Mary and said, "This is the best day of my life."

Mary held her husband's hand and jokingly pulled off his wedding band, "I thought *this* was your favourite day, darling."

David smiled, "Yes, they were both fantastic, I'll never forget how scared you were walking down the aisle. We were so young. I wouldn't change anything, though?"

"You scrubbed up well and looked so handsome in your blue suit and black tie, you looked like a film star," Mary replied.

Mary and David had been in love since the day they had met; a classic love at first sight.

Tim was growing up in a small loving family. He had nothing but had everything: love, time and kindness. David made wooden toys for Tim as a child, his favourite being a castle which he played with daily. He also had lots of plastic toy soldiers – he was three when he got them all for his birthday/Christmas. All the soldiers had names; they were his family according to his innocent sensibility. He painted the soldiers' assorted colours with his paint set; this way he knew whom was who. Tim was poor but grateful for all the love he got and was incredibly happy at home. Tim would look at the pictures of two early-learning children's books every week at aged four. He was a real bookworm but showed no real interest in joining in with other children at the park or community settings. He was invited to birthday parties, but never wanted to go to any. Tim knew his comfort zone. It was around this time he learnt the alphabet; he would practice but was awfully slow at getting the letters out when speaking. When Tim was five, he learnt how to ride a bike – Grandad and Nanna Jones bought him one as a Christmas/birthday present. It was blue and had a little bell. He also had a little black helmet that he would put on. He would go up and down the garden path and he would start/stop and practise his balance. Sometimes, if he was lucky, Grandad and Dad would get their bikes out and they would all go for a ride off track – they loved to cycle in the forest and along river banks, but would never ride fast as they wanted to take in all their surroundings.

Grandad would take lots of photos of the leaves on the ground in autumn, blossom on the trees in the summer and bare trees in the winter. He loved all the nature pictures he took. Bird photography was harder, as you had to be quiet. But with his long lens, they managed to get lovely photographs of birds from far away. They would identify the collection later with help of books from the library and print the pictures to frame and place on the bird wall at home. River boats was another enjoyable subject – the owners would wave as they went up or downstream. It was a fun time, lots of fantastic memories were made on these trips out.

Dad would also name the type of trees that were in the forest; they would collect conkers and pinecones, they would always take home a big bag to show Mum and Nanna. Mum loved the smell. She would fill bowls with them and then place on windowsills around the house; it was a rustic feel and she loved that. Dad would collect small sticks to use for kindling for the fire in the living room. Tim liked to place the sticks on top of one another when he reached home to see how high he could make a stick tower block. He enjoyed doing things like this, he kept busy.

When the weather was good, the men in the family would all go fishing. Tim's Dad David made a small fishing rod for his son – it was the cutest rod in the world, and so special. Off they all went to the river – it did get competitive with the adults. Tim would watch and see all the things that he needed to; he had a little stool to sit on and would have a packed lunch and flask. The fishing trips would be all day long. When he got a bite, he would get all excited – David would tell him he needed to keep quiet, as he would scare the fish away. He had a net too. He would catch a fish and Grandad would do the rest: reel it in and place the catch in the net, then slowly unhook the fish. Grandad would also take a photograph of his grandson, smiling and proud, then place the fish back in the river. Everyone had a fun time, and they would recount the day later to Mum and Nanna over their evening meal.

When he was small, the family would camp in the garden at home, just for the fun of it. They would turn the area into a small campsite: a small fire, with a big pot and kettle, bottles of water, a tent with two sleeping areas, sleeping bags and a bucket with a seat attached alongside sawdust to use as a toilet.

They would all sit around the fire singing songs. David would play the guitar, sometimes. Tim would play the harmonica – it was a fantastic time, lots of memories were made on those garden camping nights.

David would have a small bottle of rum and would pour himself a small cup full; Mum would have a port, and Tim a coke. The outdoor lifestyle appealed to them all and they looked forward to the summer nights when they could relax and get away from the TV and enjoy grass under their feet and fresh air.

School Years

Tim often stayed at his grandparents' home on both sides of his family during the school holidays. He would help with the farm at Nanna and Grandad Smith and read and bake bread with Nanna & Grandad Jones.

They also read plenty of books, which was his favourite hobby at the time.

He loved reading and was often found in a corner with his head in a remarkable story.

Tim had a stammer – he regularly got hit at school and bullied due to this, which made the problem worse.

He went through his daily routine: he would wake up at 7 am, wash and dress, eat breakfast and walk to school.

Once there, everything would change; he would feel insecure, alone and tormented – the bullies would start at break time, pushing him around and laughing at his clothes and his glasses.

Tim never told the teachers or his parents what was going on. He continued and put up with it and never fought back.

Occasionally, his parents would make comments if he had a graze or a bruise, but Tim always said it was accidental when playing sports or PE. Every day was the same.

Tim loved to be asleep, as he was always happy in his dreams. He was also happy at home or his grandparents Jones' or Smith's residence.

Tim lived for the weekends, when he could go to the farm and help with the pigs, sheep and cows; he loved the animals as they were always friendly... unlike the enemies at school. He adored his time and loved the school holidays when he would help every day and learn new skills.

In fact, Tim was turning to be a very clever young man – a good allrounder.

Tim was gifted, no doubt about that; he would write a lot as well as read, he drew well and would always be showing his colourings and sketching's to anyone who was around. He loved sitting and listening to the chit-chat of the families' activities and would ask a lot of questions. His stammer did not stop him from finding the answers to his queries. His other love was radio; he loved listening to music, especially the lyrics of the songs which would bring out lots of different emotions.

During the school years, Tim went through sad days; he was forever having his glasses pinched from his face and being called "four eyes" or "specky", or being told to "slooww dooowwwnnnn", as his stutter was always worse when he was being bullied. He used to wonder if any teachers ever saw what was going on and blatantly ignored what was happening – he often wondered what would happen if he reported to the principal about what had been happening to him! In the end, he decided to keep his head down and hope the harmful stuff would go away; he was not a troublemaker and would never want to get anyone in trouble (no matter how mean they were).

Every day, he was a target. One day, during another horrible playground break, the school bully asked him what it was like to be blind and not be able to talk. Tim just lost it – clenched his fist in a ball and punched the bully in his face, the boy ended up with a nosebleed. He was never picked on again in school; Tim succeeded in something and felt proud of himself.

When he was seven, he started copying artwork from comics and books; he especially liked to draw cars, rockets and Disney characters.

He would call himself a sketcher, he would ask his Mum and Dad if they liked his pictures, and they would always put the drawings on the wall in the hallway for visitors to look at.

Obviously, they were biased as the drawings were special to them.

Tim continued getting through lots of notebooks, paper, writing pads and whatever he could get his hands on to draw – he even sketched on old rolls of wallpaper he found in the understairs cupboard.

When he was ten, the school ran a competition for the ten best drawings for his school year – the winning pictures would be on display in the patients' rooms at the local hospice; everyone was excited, the two subjects were a bowl of fruit and wildlife.

Tim spent two weeks on his two pieces of art and the results were outstanding.

One of a Bengal tiger sleeping peacefully.

One of an exotic bowl of fruit.

The competition had 70 drawings in all from the pupils in his school year and the winners would be announced on the Friday (it was currently Wednesday). Tim was so nervous and excited; he bit all his nails off both hands – much to his dad's disgust.

Friday came, and the winners were announced in assembly; not only had Tim got one through to the final ten, but he got both.

He was ecstatic and nothing could take the smile off his face.

As the school years went by, Tim's grades were always excellent, he continued to learn and took in every word the teachers said in the class.

He would visit the library and would spend most of his after-school time reading poetry, old manuscripts, novels, biographies... anything and everything. Tim was a sponge and he lived to learn something new every day and remember it.

He was getting gold stars in school as his work was outstanding, and his school attendance was 100%; now that the bullying had stopped, he was doing well.

Obviously, there was always a bit of jealousy and Tim was now called "swot", "teacher's pet", and "nerd". He just laughed it off – he was a big boy now, plus he had new trendy glasses and a fashionable haircut. He was now choosing his own clothes too.

As Tim went through the years, his dad would always make a present for his birthday/Christmas out of wood. Everything was kept in the garage. Tim had photographs of all his gifts on a pinboard in his bedroom and in his scrapbook; he also had the dates and years written down.

Aged 3 – castle, 1996. One of the first things my dad made. This was made from lightweight wood and painted with three assorted colours to form a brick design, the top part of the castle had a saw-tooth pattern all around, the middle was open, my toy soldiers lived here.

Aged 4 – easel, 1997. I used the easel all the time, either with chalks or paints. I loved the smell of the paints and all the different colours. It was always messy so Mum said I must always wear an apron. A lot of my artwork is framed and hung in the spare bedroom for guests to look at.

Aged 5 – sword and shield, 1998. Another great toy. Dad painted the shield with a red cross. I used to attack the cushions in the living room, covering myself with the shield. The best practise was on grandad's farm, stacking the hay bales high and plunging the wooden sword in. I always seemed to get told off when playing with my sword and shield.

Aged 6 – drawing desk, 1999. This was a step up from the stand-up easel. I had my own desk with a drawer for my paper and a big pot to put my crayons, felt pens, colouring pencils and normal pencils. I loved my choice of several types of drawing instruments.

Aged 7 – board game: draughts, 2000. Dad worked hard at this one, it took ages to get all the squares the exact size. He told me it took weeks to make, and he was always working on it when I had gone to bed. He bought the counters in town, 12 black and 12 white. I would play this with Dad for hours every night, sometimes winning.

Aged 8 – Go-kart, 2001. A fantastic present, this was so much fun. I could pedal this and it would go forwards and backwards. It had a steering wheel so the vehicle could go left right or straight. The only problem was stopping it which was always interesting.

Aged 9 – skateboard, 2002. I'll never forget this present as it seemed dangerous at the time. I put on a small helmet and wore kneepads when I used this and it took a while to get my balance and stand on it, let alone doing any tricks. I found a smooth path and with one foot on the ground pushed away, the skateboard went flying in the air and I landed on my backside and my hands stung from the grazes. No one told me I shouldn't play with my skateboard in the rain. after a few weeks practising I was pretty good if I say so myself.

Aged 10 – football table, 2003. Once I got to 11, he wanted clothes and shoes instead; he wanted to look good.

At 12, Tim's parents bought him his first razor. His Dad, David, would show him how to lather up and slowly move the razor in the direction that the hair grows, slow and steady rinsing off the blade after each stroke, not to press too hard and avoid cutting your skin; the result was smooth skin. After that, he applied aftershave and felt all grown up.

Teen Years

Tim worked hard and got good grades as he went through his school years. He made a friend in a girl on the neighbouring farm called Jennifer – her parents owned Jacobs Farm.

Jennifer was the same age as Tim; she was a gentle soul with an older brother by ten years. She and Tim used to swap books and spend time listening to music together – they even both wrote a Christmas song for fun, later adding the music to it; they would sing it from the top of their voices and laugh aloud, holding their bellies. Also, they would have tears rolling down their face. These were the best times ever. As both born in December, they were bonded by being the same birth sign.

They used to help each other with chores, too; Tim loved communicating with Jennifer and felt relaxed in her company, so did not stammer as much (if at all).

Tim had regularly gone to the river over the years, always fishing with his dad. He was now quite a good angler; he still had the rod his dad had made, but he also had a mini collection, too. He took Jennifer sometimes on a Saturday – she would read and do quiz books lying on a rug while Tim concentrated hard, hoping to impress his girlfriend with his skills. It was peaceful and away from everyone else they knew.

Tim's stammer was not absent but it also was not bad these days. He was relaxed and did not worry about things so much. He had his trendy clothes, haircut and glasses – he felt good about himself.

He joined Jennifer on the rug, as she was stuck on a question in the quiz book. He had his arm around her, they looked into each other's eyes and both kissed.

When Tim was 15, his parents sat him down and said they had something important to say to him. He sat down and heard the news of his adoption – at once, he went into a deep shock as he had no idea or clue that he was born to a different couple; he felt so sad that his family and grandparents was not his by blood. He was upset and vowed when he was old enough, he would find them and get to know his history – he was only told snippets, which was information from the original adoption paperwork. Suddenly, he felt different, he ran straight over to see Jennifer.

He told her the story while sobbing and breathing fast, he felt the saddest he had ever been in his life. Jennifer took his hand and reassured him that she was always going to be there for him.

If he ever felt sad or happy, then, either way, she would be there; she told him he was special as he had been chosen, she gave him a big cuddle and handed him her chunky silver chain bracelet and said, "If you ever feel lonely or lost, then touch the bracelet and think of our friendship." Tim went home feeling much better about himself after offloading to his best friend.

Jacobs' Farm, which belonged to Jennifer's parents needed to have a new barn built as a storm had damaged the roof and it leaked. Additionally, the sides were constantly being repaired; it was way past its best. Tim went over to help with emptying it. A lot of the items were moved into an area next to the house. During this time, Tim noticed a tent; he talked to Jennifer's father, Bob, about his camping garden nights and told him how much fun it was. Bob said the tent was no longer used by the family and he was welcome anytime to borrow it. Tim mentioned it to Jennifer over a cup of tea later, she said "Let's do it this Friday."

Friday arrived; the tent was put up in Bob Jacobs' Garden. Bob's wife, Julia, decided to do a BBQ at the same time, so a jolly time was had; the food consisted of chicken drumsticks, sausages, beef burgers, beans and rolls with cold drinks for everyone. Bob had a small radio on with Johnny Cash playing and a pack of playing cards; it was a little different from his nights camping with his parents, but fun all the same. Jennifer and Tim would be trusted to sleep in the tent in their own sleeping bags, which they did, and they chatted all night about life, his adoption and the future… the future looked bright.

Tim and Jennifer continued for a few years enjoying each other's company, they used to see each other every day; they were falling in love.

When Jennifer was 17, her parents decided to go on holiday for a week by the coast. They would book a chalet in a resort nearby. Also in the area was a theme park so Jennifer asked Tim if he would like to come along too. It was "absolutely yes" from Tim, he loved Jennifer and the family but had never experienced a holiday of any kind; he was so excited. Jake, Bob and Judy's son would run the farm with his friend, Emma, and they had booked a week off work from the hospital.

He went home and told his parents about his plans for the following day; they were ecstatic. Tim started looking in his wardrobe for nice clothing to take. He decided to take seven t-shirts, seven pairs of boxer shorts, seven pairs of socks, two pairs of shorts, two tracksuit bottoms, two shirts and two trousers, two jumpers, swimming trunks, one pair of shoes and one pair of trainers plus a coat.

They would leave on Saturday and come back the following Saturday. The journey would take two hours and they could check in at 2 pm. They left Jacobs' farm at 11 am and all the cases were in the boot of the car along with a few boxes of food and drinks.

Bob got behind the wheel and shouted in the back to Tim, "Would you like to choose the first CD for the journey? There is a file full of them on the seat."

Tim flicked through the choices and chose *Queen's Greatest Hits.* He passed the CD to Julia who inserted it into the player saying, "Great choice Tim. One of my favourites of all time."

It had been raining when they first set off but now the sun was out and the sky was blue with a few white clouds. It was very warm too. Tim was wearing his blue t-shirt with back shorts; he liked to be casual. He had a blue baseball cap on to match his top, his white trainers were just a few weeks old and still a bit tight. He looked good. Jennifer wore a long summer dress with sunglasses and straw hat. She looked stunning, her hair was flowing around her shoulders, and she wore a silver necklace with a cross on it. She was clicking her fingers to the song. Tim laughed, and Julia and Bob also joined in. It was like the scene in the film *Wayne's World* with the characters singing *Bohemian Rhapsody.*

Tim wanted to capture this moment, he rummaged in his bag for his camera, and then took a few snaps from the back of the car of Jennifer and her parents. One of many he would take on the trip as he was a keen photographer.

The journey was going well and the CD was finished. It was now Jennifer's turn to pick and she chose *The Very Best of Fleetwood Mac*, even though Tim and Jennifer were half their parents' age, they knew the music. The CD would take them right to the destination.

As they all pulled into the car park, Jennifer grabbed Tim's hand. She was smiling. Bob parked outside to check the cabin while Julia gathered her booking paperwork. She opened the door and felt the warmth of the May sunshine; it was gorgeous with blue sky and a few fluffy clouds. Bob high-fived his wife saying, "Let's do this," and then laughed out loud. Julia ran to the check-in desk where the receptionist gave her the directions to the accommodation and a site map. Julia picked up the key for their home for the next week.

Back in the car, she looked at the map and told Bob to keep going straight up the road to the end and then turn left. The chalet was the last one in the row, number eight. Bob parked outside. It was impressive, a nice thick tidy hedge separated them from number nine. It was private and had a nice grassy area to the side with steps going to the door and, more importantly, lots of sun.

They all went inside, lots of light filled the interior, lots of windows filled the space with sunshine, the kitchen dining room and lounge were open plan, with two leather sofas, a massive TV, Wi-Fi, a lovely wooden table and six chairs, one double bedroom and two single ones. They bought the bags in from the car and placed the two boxes of food on the table. Bob opened the patio doors which led to a decked area with hot tub. This place was amazing like a lottery win. What a great break the next seven days would be.

Julia started putting the food away. She had noticed a small shop on the site so would go and buy milk, bread, cheese, coke, wine and a few beers.

Jennifer asked her dad if he minded if her and Tim went into the hot tub. She was so excited as she had never been in one, the answer was yes. Tim went into his room with his bag, his towel was already on the bed folded up by the maid who had cleaned the chalet earlier on that day. He picked it up and it smelt fresh.

Jennifer shouted through the door to Tim: "Are you ready yet?" The door opened and there stood her boyfriend in his purple shorts with a towel under his arm. Jennifer had her orange patterned swimsuit on. She looked older than 17, and womanly. They walked outside. Bob had opened the lid for them they both stepped inside and the temperature was perfect. They pressed the button and the swirling started, lovely jets massaged their backs when they sat down. Julia was back from the shop and put two glasses of Coke on the table next the teens.

She put the kettle on to make coffee for her and her husband. They went outside to check their surroundings; it was so peaceful Bob thought he could hear the sea. Julia said they should go for a walk in a while and check out the area and surroundings. Bob liked that idea.

Bob and Julia drank their coffee, ate cheese and biscuits and then went off exploring. The both had flip flops and shorts on. Hand in hand, they walked out of the site and towards the sea. The beach had pebbles and a slight breeze. It was fairly busy as it was Saturday; families with young children paddling in the water and a few jet-skis were in the distance. Bob found a seat and they both sat down. This is the life, no animals, no stress just peace and quiet. Julia looked around; there were a few stalls selling beach wear, buckets and spades and drinks, bike hire, plus toilets, a small café and an ice cream van. Bob went towards it, queued for five mins and came back with two cones. The sun was still as hot as when they had arrived. Julia got the sarong out of her bag and wrapped it around her waist. She didn't want to get burnt. She had forgotten to put sun cream on before going out and her legs were turning pink. Bob had forgotten his sunglasses. He was trying to talk Julia into handing hers over but no chance. She laughed at how disorganised they had been rushing out for a walk.

They got back to the chalet and Jennifer and Tim were both sunbathing at the front of the accommodation, lying on their wet towels, listening to music on a small battery radio, a bottle of sun cream next to them, sunglasses, and hats; the youngsters were more organised that the adults.

When it got to 6 pm, everyone was starting to get hungry. Julia and Bob were going to the supermarket on Sunday to get more groceries for the week, but before that they needed to all eat. Fish and chips was the evening meal everyone wanted. They would all eat in so the foursome made their way to Fishy Things and there was no queue which was handy. The waitress showed them all to a table near the window; it was the last seat in the restaurant. Bob asked the waitress, Holly, for the drinks menu. She went off and was back quickly with this and a dessert menu too. Everyone knew they were having cod, chips and mushy peas. Tim choose lemonade, Jennifer wanted a diet coke, Bob and Julia had a ginger beer each. As Holly went off to get the drinks, Jennifer reached into her pocket and pulled out her mobile phone. She wanted to check her weather app and plan her trip according to the forecast. Sunday, Monday, Tuesday, Wednesday was looking like pure sunshine; meanwhile, Thursday was cloudy, and Friday rain – not bad at all.

Holly came back with the drinks and straws. Tim sucked on the straw and felt the cold liquid go straight to his brain – brain freeze. He would not do that again so quickly. Everyone laughed.

Bob wanted to go out on Sunday after shopping to the nearest town. There was a castle, a river with hire boats, lots of shops and a hop on hop on bus. It was all settled, they would leave the chalet at 12 pm and go for the short drive. Julia wanted to go on a boat trip up the river and back, while Tim and Jennifer were keen on the bus trip. Bob was happy visiting the castle as he loved history.

Holly came to the table with the food; the fish was crispy and hot and it tasted crunchy and then soft. The chips were cooked to perfection. Holly also bought out tartare sauce, vinegar and salt and pepper.

Bob took a taste of his cod, and said, "Oh, wow, the fish always tastes better when at the coast. How delicious is this meal!"

They all nodded in agreement and the rest of the meal was demolished in silence as everyone enjoyed dinner.

Everyone chose apple pie and ice cream for dessert. Holly took away the plates and Bob paid the bill and left a tip. They all got up and walked out of the door full to the brim.

The chalet was not far away they went back. The sun was still out. Julia asked Bob if he fancied going to the clubhouse that evening. "Absolutely yes!" he said, "I'm going to wear my new jeans." He smiled and continued, "Life is to short, let's have fun. It's not often we have a chance to go away."

At the clubhouse later that evening, Tim and Jennifer went straight to the arcade. They hadn't been in one before. All the machines were lit and all the noise was coming from everywhere, from coins going in and coming out and handles being pulled. Tim went up to the kiosk and handed over £10, he then handed Jennifer half of it.

"Which machine do you fancy going on first?" he asked. It was overwhelming.

"I'm not sure," Jennifer replied.

Tim liked the idea of the seated racing car machine so he sat down and read the instructions and he pushed the coin into the slot. As he did, the game came to life. Jennifer watched amazed and grinned. Tim got quite a good score. He enjoyed the race so much he vowed to play every night and do better every time.

Jennifer walked towards a space invader machine; left, right, up and down, this arcade was so much fun. They spent the rest of the time on playing table football together; Jennifer winning 6–10. They got themselves a coke each from the vending machine and started looking for Bob and Julia.

Jennifer turned to Tim, "I am so glad you said yes to coming away with us. It wouldn't have been the same without you." Tim loved hearing this, he grabbed her hand and gave it a squeeze and replied, "I'm glad too."

The pair found Bob and Julia who were both sitting near the back. They were all tired so they decided to walk back to the chalet, Bob whistling all the way home, everyone happy after a great first day.

Day two, waking up with no alarm is just the best. Everyone slept in until 9. Julia went to make morning tea, Tim showered, dressed then joined everyone on the sofas. He had decided on a tracksuit today and trainers for comfort. It sounded like a busy day ahead. Jennifer was in her pyjamas and slippers, her blonde hair tied back in a ponytail. She was beautiful without makeup and posh clothes, very natural with clear skin and bright blue eyes. She had great energy.

Bob and his wife were both dressed and ready to go to the supermarket. They had written a list so as not to forget anything. They drank down their mugs of earl grey and headed for the car.

"We won't be long," said Julia.

Tim took his camping chair and went to the front of the chalet to see if there were any birds in the hedges. He could hear them so he grabbed his camera and set it up. He wanted to get a few pictures if the timing was right so he sat behind the tripod sipping his tea and looking through the lens. He scattered bird seed on the ground and sat in wait; a few sparrows and a robin landed on the grass and Tim clicked away. As soon as the food was gone the birds disappeared. Tim checked the photos on the camera. "Not bad," he was pleased with the quality of the robin it was like a painting with a green canvas.

Bob drove his car into the parking place, he had most of the food for the week ahead burgers and rolls, salad stuff, fruit, potatoes, pies, vegetables, chicken, stuffing, bread, cheese, ham, pork pie, crisps, milk, eggs, cereal and juice.

Julie started making everyone ham and cheese rolls; she wrapped them in clingfilm and packed the food in the hamper with apples, drinks and biscuits.

"Everyone ready?" said Bob, they all marched out to the car with information on car parks and planned the day ahead.

Jennifer and Tim would be dropped off at the start of the bus tour, they would all meet up in the same place at 5 pm to go home. The tickets could be bought as they boarded the bus; the queue was long as it was midday. They wanted to sit upstairs as they both had cameras and would be able to get a good view on the top deck with no dirty windows spoiling the photos.

Tim paid for the tickets, he had always saved his birthday and Christmas money, and now was the time to enjoy it. They both ran up the steps and got a seat near the front with a bird's eye view of the city.

They put on the headphones and tuned into English, looked at the map and, with a pen, ticked the stops they wanted to get off at.

Stop 1 was the university. It was 100 years old. A stunning stone and glass building, a popular place with free admission. Jennifer did not want to get off so she took a few snaps from the bus.

Stop 2 was the town museum looking very old and grey but with a lovely cloud-free blue sky behind it. This one was free admission but asking for a small donation. They got off and went inside; it was a small museum with a few old pots and coins, old maps of the area and a few knives and medals. It was a quick visit and was able to hop onto the next bus that stopped.

Stop 3 was the castle. Tim could see Bob and Julia outside so he zoomed in with his camera and took a few long distance shots. Jennifer laughed and spoke at the same time, "Don't they look small, they also look like lovebirds holding hands. I have never see them like this as they are always working so hard."

Tim looked at his girlfriend, quietly whispered in her ear, "Hopefully, we will be like that one day."

Stop 4 was the river and bridge, this was one of the places they would jump off and have a picnic by the river. The blanket was laid; it was in the shade. They ate their food and flipped their shoes off, had a drink then laid in the sun taking in the rays.

Stop 5 was the leisure park which had two swimming pools with flume rides, waterfalls, a wave pool, a sauna and a steam room. Also in the park was a cinema and a bowling alley.

Stop 6 was a huge ice rink; a big queue of people were lined up here to get back onto the bus, all with rosy cheeks after skating for the last few hours.

Stop 7 was a bowling alley and restaurant; lots of people got off here and children only paid £1 a game.

Stop 8 was at a national trust property. Tim and Jennifer visited the garden as this was free; admission to the house was a bit expensive, the flowers and orchard were in full bloom, immaculate with not a blade of grass out of place. Jennifer had a bag of jelly beans in her pocket, she opened the pack and gave Tim half, "This is the life. I am enjoying today so much. I love your company, Tim. Do you think we will be together forever?"

Tim put his arm around her. " I hope so," he said with his eyes all shiny. They stopped at the tearoom, had a hot chocolate and ate a cake.

Stop 9, the home of a famous singing star. English country home with gates; now the singer was on the panel of a TV talent show.

Stop 10, walled gardens and nature walk; this was another good place as they could get a few steps in and a bit of photography. Jennifer posed in front of the trees and fountains, statues and wildflowers. The scenery was good and the sun was shining brightly; it was like being in heaven. Tim set up the tripod and they had a few shots together with a lovely lake in the background.

Stop 11, a coastal walk with guided tours every hour; this was another lovely walk, it took about 30 mins to walk, and the views were stunning. Tim reached for his camera, click, click, click.

Stop 12, the graveyard this is one they would give a miss.

Back at stop 1 they got off the bus as it was time to meet Bob and Judy. They found a toilet, refreshed, then waited by the seat near the car park. Judy was waving to them both trying to get their attention. Tim looked up and waved back. Bob said the castle was old and ancient, and full of character; he was talking about all the different rooms and furnishings, the armoury, the grounds of the castle, the river running through to the castle, moat and drawbridge.

They all chatted about their day all the way home – all tired but full of memories.

That evening Bob sparked up the BBQ and cooked the burgers and chicken. Jennifer chopped up a salad and put potatoes in the oven to bake, Tim was on the decking reading a thriller. Judy was reading a romance novel. Jennifer opened cold drinks from the fridge and took them outside for everyone. Bob was listening to 70s music on the radio and singing along as he turned the food over making sure everything was cooked properly. Bob didn't get a chance to cook often as he was always so busy but he enjoyed doing a BBQ in the summer evenings. The food was set on the garden table; everyone sat down, the chicken was juicy with exotic spices running through, the skin was crispy and the burgers were 100% beef. Jennifer remembered that in the fridge she had seen a pack of cheese slices. She ran to the kitchen as wanted a cheeseburger; the meal ended another successful day. Everyone stayed in to watch a film on Sunday night; the sea air was making them all tired.

Waking up on Monday, Tim wanted to check out the games room on site. He knew there were a few snooker tables, plus dart boards and table tennis. Bob also liked this idea; he liked the competitive side in Tim and challenged him to best of three on each. Judy would also play against her daughter. This would be later in the afternoon. Before that they all lazed around, eating toast, cereal, eggs and drank tea, reading and looking at the photos they had taken from the day before, all laughing at one of Tim with his hair sticking up when he jumped off a fallen tree. Tim loved being with the family, it was fun, and they had great banter with each other. The afternoon came and went quickly. Bob beat Tim at darts and Tim beat Bob at snooker and table tennis; Jennifer, on the other hand, won every game.

On the way home, they had already decided they would hire bikes for Tuesday; all of them would ride one of the bike trails they had seen on the leaflet at the hire store.

Everyone got up early, showered, dressed in their finest cycling clothes and pitched up at the cycle shop which had just opened. Bob hired four bikes. After all the checks were done and saddles and handlebars adjusted, they set off for the trail. It was one mile from where they currently were. Bob led the way with his wife behind. Tim and Jennifer next to each other at the back. The trail started next to the railway station and it was all off-road.

"Are we all ready?" asked Bob.

The trail was mainly stones and it was a bit jumpy. The tyres were crunching as they rode through the 12 miles of countryside which would lead them to a bay near the sea. The sun was out but everyone felt a bit chilly; hopefully the clouds would disappear soon. They rode through fields, past farms, back of industrial estates, leisure parks and more fields. They stopped halfway as Jennifer had a problem with her gears getting stuck. Finally, they all reached the destination point; the bay was beautiful, it was fairly busy too. Boats rides were in place, kayak hire, tea rooms, stalls selling beach wear – a gem of a place. They walked the bikes to a table and sat down for a pot of tea and scone each.

Tim popped into the shop to buy a bag of sweets, a pen and three postcards with stamps. He chose one of the bay with the boats, one of the cottages around the bay and another of the shops were they currently stood. He paid for his purchase. Jennifer wanted to buy fridge magnet and keyring then they walked back to the table were Tim looked at his postcards for his mum and dad, nan and grandad Jones and Smith. He missed them all but was having such a great time; it was a lovely adventure for him. Bob looked at this watch; it was lunchtime.

"Does anyone fancy all day breakfast?" They were serving it at the café; it was a bargain at £3.99 a head. Judy fancied scrambled eggs on toast with a side of bacon, Jennifer was salivating at sausage and beans with crumpets, the men had the full English breakfast, hashbrowns, sausage, bacon, tomatoes, beans, mushrooms, eggs with hot buttered toast on the side. Tim thought his belly would burst while Bob said he felt pregnant and they all laughed. Judy said he would have to ride harder on the way back to burn it off.

They stayed at the bay for another hour taking in the scenery. Bob bought a newspaper and Judy read her book. Jennifer pulled out a picnic rug and laid down and closed her eyes. Tim started taking more photos for his photo album he would make later. Eventually they had to cycle back to the resort; it took longer as there had been a drain problem behind the industrial estate and water was everywhere. Judy fell sideways off her bike and her new trainers were covered in sludge; they were ruined. She was so upset as she loved her orange trainers. They eventually got back exhausted so they went to the chalet and had a cold drink. At this point they all jumped in the jacuzzi to relax and plan what they would do that evening.

Wednesday arrived. *Another blue sky, and more birds to be photographed,* thought Tim. They all had porridge as Judy had made a big pan for them all.

"Morning, Tim," said Judy as she handed him a hot mug of tea.

"Hhhello," stammered Tim, "did yyou sleep well?"

"Fine," said Judy, "It looks like another good day weatherwise, I like the look of this walking tour. What do you think?"

"It starts at midday and its run by the local hiking group."

"Yes," replied Tim, "that looks good."

He sat down at the table next to Jennifer; Bob was on the opposite side. The porridge was steaming in the bowls.

"I have blueberries to add if anyone would like fruit in their porridge," said Judy, "and sugar if anyone would like a sprinkling on top."

After breakfast, Judy rang the tour to find out if there were any spaces; luckily there was. She prepaid on her bank card then set a timer an hour before the tour on her mobile phone. She stretched out on the sofa with her book. Bob washed the dishes while Jennifer showered. Tim went outside with his camera; it was all very chilled out.

Tim wrote his postcards.

Dear Mum and Dad,

I am having a brilliant holiday with Jennifer and her parents. The weather is hot and the chalet very modern. We have a hot tub outside. We went on a sightseeing trip and a bike ride. Lots to see and do.

See you on Saturday.

Love,

Tim.

He wrote the same to both of his grandparents and fixed the stamps in place, He then went to his room and started packing his backpack for the walk, drink, sweets, banana, sandwich and crisps; not forgetting the post cards as he had seen a post-box just outside the resort.

It was time to leave the resort for their walk. Bob was checking his room for his walking boots and Judy and Jennifer were ready to go. They locked the chalet and made their way to the front of the pub outside the site; a few others had gathered.

The walk itself had a category of three to four hours and easy, moderate hills, with a stop in two hours at a country pub for lunch which was supplied in the price with a soft drink.

Jennifer had cleaned her not-so-orange trainers; they were good for hills. Tim had walking shoes too. They were new and tight on his feet. He had put a thick pair of socks on for comfort. The guide introduced herself. Her name was Wendy and she lived in the area, her nickname was Wednesday Wendy. She laughed as she said in winter it was changed to Windy Wendy.

The group was ready and numbered 15 walkers in total; all of them had a drink to sip, the group was given energy bar too in case they felt tired, the weather was cloudy but warm. Off they marched in a bundle, listening to the commentary from Wendy about the history of the village, how old the beautiful thatched cottages were, how the pond was formed and the different sorts of ducks who frequent it. They walked towards the water mill and heard all about that, onwards and upwards, up a slight incline to a nature reserve with different birds. Tim enjoyed this and his camera was back out taking snaps. Past the church on the right then down towards the pub for lunch everyone was having fish and chips.

Bob laughed and said loudly, "Again, that's twice in a few days." Just as well he loved it.

The group were from all around the UK, all holidaying in the area staying in air B&Bs, lodges, campsites and the resort; everyone was in a good mood. After food and drinks the tour continued up the hill to a row of independent shops where the group could buy souvenirs, up to the top of the hill with stunning views across the country, then back past the poppy field and ½ mile back to the starting point. Tim's feet hurt from his new boots, he could not wait to take them off. They all spent the evening eating, playing board games and watching movies on a film channel before going to bed.

Tim woke up to the sound of rain on the chalet roof; he looked out of the window, which was next to his bed and the ground was sodden. It had been heavy rain over night. He put his radio on and placed the headphones on his head and snuggled deeper into his duvet; it was nice and snug in bed. He looked at his watch and it was 7am; too early to get up and make a drink. He sipped on his water bottle next to his bed, closed his eyes and relaxed.

He must have fallen asleep as next thing he knew there was a tap on his door. It was 9:15 am and everyone was up and chatting at the table drinking hot tea. Bob passed a mug to Tim, then Bob looked out the front door as he heard a car alarm making a noise; it wasn't his.

Bob looked at Tim and said: "Do you fancy coming to the facilities onsite shortly? They have a gym I like the look of."

Tim looked at Bob. He was healthy and fit, Tim probably could keep up with him.

"Hmmm, yes, I have never been to one before. Bbbbut I will give it a go."

Bob smiled, "That's the attitude Tim, we can have a sauna after too. The weather isn't great so it'll be a stay home kind of day today." The girls would stay in the chalet, have a hot tub, watch morning tv and have breakfast ready for the boys on their return.

Bob and Tim packed a bag each and wasted no time getting to the gym. They checked in, filled their bottles with water and checked the place out; it had so many pieces of equipment, weights, lifting machines, bikes, running machines, mats, hand weights and classes you could book. Aerobics was currently taking place with yoga next at 10. Bob decided to warm up on the running machine. He set the timer and programme and was off. Tim went for the ski machine. It was fairly busy with music pounding out of the speakers. Tim had a view out of the window as he worked out to dance music. Bob was next to him, he was asking Tim about his adoption and his thoughts.

Tim explained saying: "I had no idea. Not a clue. I think I went into shock. It was a bad dream; Mum was crying and Dad had his arm around her. They said I was the best thing to happen to them in their lives. We all cried then and they promised nothing would change, but I do feel a bit different now."

Bob said he understood adding, "If you ever want to chat, Tim, we are here, no hesitations, ok?"

They both went on to lift weights badly. Tim then went on the rowing machine while Bob decided on a pull down weight machine; both were sweating at this point so they decided to change and have a sauna. The hot steam was overwhelming. Tim had gone in with his glasses and couldn't see a thing; he went back to the lockers and placed the glasses inside and joined Bob for the final ten mins in the sauna laughing. He still couldn't see a thing.

When the boys got back to the chalet they could smell the bacon cooking under the grill. They were starving. It was 10:30 but it seemed like they had been up for hours and done so much. Jennifer toasted sourdough bread then smothered it in butter. Judy was also cooking mushrooms, tomatoes and eggs.

"Hey, let's dish up, the boys look hungry. Good timing. Sit down and we will serve you." said Judy. The breakfast hit the spot and orange juice was served too.

"Does anyone want any more toast?" asked Bob, "I am going to have one more slice." Breakfast was finished and it was free time; no plans were in place so everyone could do their own thing.

Jennifer fancied a walk into the town as she had to get a present for her brother for looking after the farm.

"Good idea," said Judy opening her purse. She passed a couple of £5 notes to her daughter and said to buy something nice.

Judy picked up her book. She wanted to finish it by tomorrow evening. Bob started flicking through the channels of the TV. The youngsters had grabbed their coat and brollies they would be walking to town. They had been near to it yesterday on the hike so knew where to go. They wouldn't be too long, as soon as they left Bob cuddled up to his wife. She didn't look up from her book; she enjoyed the quality time they had together.

She spoke softly, "Two more days, hun. Hasn't it gone quickly? How was the workout?"

"Ahhh," said Bob, "It was nice. Tim is such a lovely boy. So grown up for his age and a clever lad too. We did chat about his recent bombshell of being adopted. I think he will be fine as he is so grounded."

"I do hope so," said Judy, "he's got us to support him if he feels lost, sometimes it's nice to talk outside of your own bubble. He is shy but coming out of his shell. I can see Jennifer likes him a lot."

Meanwhile, Tim and Jennifer had been in a few shops looking at the different gifts on offer; eggs cups with names on, wallets, keyrings, mugs, lots of ornaments, cheap tacky bits and bobs. They laughed at some of the items on display. Jennifer decided on a cheese board set and a pair of socks each with their names on them. Jake in blue and Emma in pink. They bought a bag of mints and more bird seed. Tim asked Jennifer to wait for him outside as he wanted to buy something for his mum and dad; he chose a rolling pin for Mum as she loves pastry making, and a pack of cards for Dad, his were at least ten years old and falling apart. He cheekily picked up a pair of socks for his girlfriend with her name on to match the ones she had already purchased.

They walked home to find Bob and Judy fast asleep on the sofa with the TV on and they laughed.

That afternoon they watched TV, and played board games. Dinner was a pork pie, cheese with ham salad, with beers for the adults and shandy for the youngsters. Very quickly it was getting late. Tim asked Jennifer if she wanted to go in the hot tub.

"Is the pope catholic?" was the reply. They grabbed their fluffy dressing gowns and flip flops, then opened the patio doors; the sky was clear, all the stars were twinkling. Tim had taken his radio outside, he put on classic hits, they stepped into the warm swirling bubbles, Jennifer's hair was tied up in a bun and she looked beautiful with her fresh skin, long eyelashes and cute smile. Tim held her hand he looked at his girlfriend and told her he loved her.

Friday arrived. Jennifer had slept well and Tim could not believe he had told his girlfriend he loved her as it had just came out in the romantic moment, he meant every word though. Everyone was up and dressed and it was another free day.

"Hmmm, what does everyone want to do today?" said Bob. He had already planned to go and play golf with his wife.

Jennifer looked at her dad and said, "Well, we fancied crazy golf. Tim was talking about it yesterday and we thought it would be a fun day with swimming afterwards."

"Perfect, all settled then," said Judy, "we can all meet up at four or five. We want to go to the clubhouse tonight for bingo at seven, then a tribute act is booked for the hall at eight, then karaoke until midnight or a disco in the pub next door; whatever we feel like later on." It sounds like a plan.

Tim and Jennifer left the chalet at the same time as Bob and Judy, "See you later," shouted Tim, "have fun."

Tim paid for them both and they got their putters. The small crazy golf course was 18 holes. Slopes and hills were all over the course and a few of the putts were rubbish and should have gone in, but overall, they were both rubbish. Off they went to the pool.

Jennifer looked at Tim and said, "Did you mean what you said last night in the hot tub?"

Tim looked at his girlfriend and replied, "I have never been so certain of anything in my life. You make me so happy. I get on well with your parents and brother. I love spending my time with you; this holiday has made me realise what a connection we have."

They held hands and skipped over to the pool grinning. Once changed, they met outside the pool entrance and walked towards the medium pool with the slides. The water was cold and Tim splashed his girlfriend and she splashed him right back.

"Stop, Tim, I'm not ready yet. I'm not used to the sudden cold temperature."

Tim was a good swimmer. He sunk down into the water and started swimming the length of the pool. Once at the other side, he bobbed up turned and waved and Jennifer waved back. She was now in the water properly with just her head sticking out, she swam over to join Tim. Jennifer asked to use Tim's googles as the chlorine made her eyes pink, both went on the slides, did a few pool widths, then sat on the side chatting in the water.

"I've had a lovely holiday. Thank you for inviting me. I can't tell you how much fun it has been. We should do this every year from now on." He put his arm around Jennifer's shoulders and said, "One day, I'll pay and take your parents away."

After the swim, they both dried and went for a hot chocolate in the café. They had time to pass. It was before four Bob and Judy wouldn't be back yet. They decided to go outside the resort and walk on the beach. Tim bought sticks of rock and biscuits as gifts to take home the following day; he had missed his parents but not that much.

The lovebirds walked back to the chalet. Bob's car was outside, they opened the door and went in.

"Asleep again," said Jennifer laughing aloud.

Judy had made a shepherd's pie earlier that morning. She heated the oven and placed it on the rack; dinner was going to be in 40 minutes.

After dinner, the foursome headed to the bingo hall; Jennifer and Bob bought a book and waited for the numbers to be called out, the youngsters went back to the arcade. They had a few pounds left to play with, both of them played asteroids. Bob walked in a while later to say the tribute act would be on shortly, they were now sitting on a table near the front. Bob bought his wife a large wine, he got himself a Guinness, plus two cokes and a few bags of peanuts.

The tribute act was great and had quite a few people dancing on the wooden floor in front of the stage. Bob sang along as he knew the songs. Tim took photos of them all, Judy grabbed the camera and took pictures of the lovebirds; they did look good together, both photogenic too.

Around 10, it was announced that karaoke would be on.

"This will be fun," said Tim, "usually it is people who can't sing well that go on stage said Bob."

"You better put your name down then," said Judy laughing.

Bob did get up and sing a Frank Sinatra number to a round of applause. He was chuffed to bits. Jennifer wanted to do a duet with Tim but he couldn't, so Bob joined his daughter and they sang *Islands in the Stream* by Kenny Rogers and Dolly Parton. Judy had tears in her eyes.

They all walked home; it started to drizzle but it did not matter as nothing would spoil a momentous week away.

In the morning the alarm went off at 8:30; they had 1.5 hours to eat breakfast, pack and clean. They had cereal plus juice for breakfast as it was quick, they then got everything packed in the car. They still had food left which was amazing.

"Right," said Bob, "I'm choosing the music." He put on Frank Sinatra's *Greatest Hits.* Judy picked a country and western CD for the next one.

The car pulled up at the farm at midday. "Thank you so much for letting me join you all," said Tim, "I've had the best time, it's been fffun."

Jennifer smiled and said, "See you later, Tim. Thank you for joining us. See you after dinner."

Tim pointed to the bag on the seat, "A little present for you." She opened the bag and grinned.

"Ha-ha, thank you, a pair of socks, that's funny. I will wear them later." She blew Tim a kiss.

When Tim left school at 17, he would help his dad with his carpentry work they would make bespoke furniture, fit kitchens and build sheds. They also built unique table and chairs out of pine wood. Although he loved this, he did not see it as a future career. This was just a stop gap. He would talk to his dad about his adoption – he found out his mother could not have children. She had always wanted a big family but after trying for ten years, she visited the GP; the doctor ran tests, the conclusion was she would never naturally have her own baby. David had consoled Mary every month for years – Tim had changed their lives. Tim never spoke to his Mum about the adoption as she would feel upset and emotional.

Adult

On Christmas day in 2011, it was Tim's 18th. Bob, Julia, Jennifer and Tim's parents would take Tim to the pub for the first drink as an adult; he chose a whisky as did not know what else to have. He took a mouthful and it burnt his throat. He winced and everyone laughed! After that, Tim stuck to beer and quite liked the taste, too. Jennifer was 18 a few weeks later.

They all had a turkey dinner with all the trimming, then recounted tales of the past. They all went home a little drunk, but grateful for their fortunes and their great lives (a few still wearing a paper hat from the cracker on the walk home).

On a Friday night out in the nearby pub a few weeks later Tim and Jennifer decided to find out a bit more about each other.

Tim started the chat, "What is the most embarrassing thing that has ever happened to you?"

Jennifer thought hard, sipped on her Bacardi and Coke, looked at Tim and replied, "When I was eight, I was accidentally knocked into a swimming pool. I could not swim and nearly drowned and I was pulled out the water and was breathing heavily. Getting my breath back was hard and I panicked. Even though I was scared, I felt embarrassed because everyone was looking at me." Jennifer laughed and blushed at the same time. "After that I learnt to swim, so it would never happen again. So, I will ask you the same question Tim."

Tim looked at Jennifer and said: "It was probably when I was at school, and I used to get bullied. I found that embarrassing because I had to stick up for myself. I am quite shy. I hate the fact had I had not done anything wrong but was getting picked on for my looks. Being a child is so hard, if someone does not like you, you can become a target of hate over nothing." Jennifer agreed entirely with what Tim was saying, she held his hand. Tim picked up his drink with his other hand and quickly drank half of it.

Next question said Tim, "If you could have dinner with anyone dead or alive who would it be?"

Jennifer loved film and music so it was hard to choose just one and she went for one of each. "Whitney Houston and Tom Cruise." She went on to say she could choose from at least ten. Tim's turn to answer, "Johnny Depp and David Bowie."

Now a few hours had gone by, the conversation got deeper as the drinks flowed; they were getting flirty laughing a lot.

Jennifer asked Tim what the worst chat up line he had used on a girl. Going slightly red and wiping his glasses with a tissue, he explained that he had never had the courage to chat to the ladies, not that he knew any other females as he was a private person.

Jennifer apologised and then changed the subject; the drink had made her tongue loose.

"Tim, what does your future look like and what are your dreams and plans?"

"Oh, I have many plans, I dream of lots of things out of my reach; one minute I want to be a marine biologist the next an airline pilot. My mind is always in overdrive and I find it hard to switch off. But I do want a happy life, have enough money without worrying and a few children, at least two, a boy and girl would be great."

Jennifer squeezed Tim hand, "I want exactly the same."

At this point Tim stood up to go to the bar to get another round of drinks in.

Tim decided when he was 19 he wanted to drive; his mum and dad had saved hard for the first 10 driving lessons with a local company called Youdrive. The driver, Jono turned up at 9 am on a sunny Sunday morning for the first lesson. Tim showed his licence and filled in a bit of paperwork. The driver went through the basics, first, second, third, fourth and fifth gear, handbrake, steering wheel, mirrors especially the side ones, lights, etc. The car was a small Ford Fiesta and Jono drove them both to a quiet road about a mile away to practise. Luckily for Tim being early on Sunday most people were still in bed. Tim and Jono swapped places. Tim started the car up and after a few kangaroo hops he quickly learnt about clutch control. He apologised then laughed out loud. Jono had seen it all before. Tim stayed calm, then carried on straight up the road slowly changing into second, third and fourth, never getting to fifth. All the time Jono would explain the importance of the mirrors and indicating before making any moves. The lesson went well and was over in a flash, another lesson was booked for the following Sunday at the same time. Tim's dad had already mentioned that Mary's car was no longer being used. This would be given to Tim if he wanted to use it for himself. The car was a red mini, obviously the

48

answer was a big yes. Tim immediately started cleaning it inside and out, he put his favourite things in the boot; camping cooker, kettle, tent, plus his fishing stuff, much to his dad's amusement.

Sunday came around quickly. Tim was waiting on the doorstep for Jono. The car pulled up, Tim got in and put his seatbelt on. They both did their pleasantries and off they went; same as last week, first, second, third and fourth never going into fifth as they were going very slow, Tim was practising the gears, checking mirrors, indicating, parking, stopping and starting. The lesson went well and Jono was happy too. The following weekend, Tim would have two lessons, a two-hour driving session. Every week went by quickly, it was Sunday again. Jono beeping outside for Tim to join him. The lessons were smooth, Tim was a good driver, never being told when to change gear. The instructor only had to tell him where to go.

Jono turned to Tim and said, "I think you're ready for your test. We will get you booked in." Tim had passed the theory test a few months back so he was excited. He had been using his savings to pay for the lessons since the original ten ran out and he was in such a good mood when he got out of the car. He thanked Jono and ran to let his parents know the good news.

The test was booked for the following Saturday at 10 am. Tim could not sleep the night before, going through everything in his head, telling himself that he has got this.

Jono turned up and patted Tim on the back, "I have every confidence in you, Tim. You are one of my best pupils. They both arrived at the test centre. Tim filled in his paperwork and then it was time. The lesson was going well until Tim was asked to reverse back around a corner. Tim reversed too far away from the kerb and he instantly presumed he had failed. He apologised then did it again without a prompt – perfect. The lesson carried on until they returned to the centre. Jono immediately grabbed Tim's hand and shook it saying, "Congratulations, you have passed."

"Ohhh, thank you, I am so happy," said Tim grinning from ear to ear. When Tim got home, he passed his good news on to his mum and both of his grandparents who were all waiting patiently. Dad sang loudly, "For he's a jolly good fella," and they all laughed. Dad then got on the phone to the insurance company to get Tim's car insurance sorted out.

Tim went out to the car and he asked his parents if they wanted a lift to the shops, or the river, anywhere they wanted to go. He just wanted to get behind the wheel so they all decided to take a drive up the duel carriage way to the next town and back; not to get out and spend any money but to get Tim used to the car. They also stopped at a garage where tyre pressures were checked – fluids and oil.

Later Tim met Jennifer, they walked to the pub to celebrate being a new driver. They chatted about this and that, the future, places to visit in the car, camping holidays were high on the list.

On Sunday, Tim went for his first drive on his own, he was nervous as he had always had someone next to him. He wanted to go on the motorway and he wondered if it was as busy as he had imagined. It turned out it wasn't; it was easier than driving through the town. Afterwards, Tim went to Jennifer's and joined her family for a cooked breakfast, bacon, eggs, beans, mushrooms, sausage and toast. It was a Sunday ritual for her family, they would also drink lots of tea and all chat. Jennifer's brother, Jake, would visit with his friend, Emma, they both worked together locally at the hospital; both nurses and diligent workers. Luckily, in their busy schedule of working days, nights and most weekends, they managed the Sundays off. It was always fun on Sundays as it was all very relaxed, afterwards was usually a walk in the countryside or doing some kind of outdoor pursuit like golf. Tim got high-fived by the whole family as he walked in.

"Well done mate, join the club," said Jake. They had bought him a new air freshener for the car plus a steering wheel cover, ice scraper and de-icer.

That evening, Tim took Jennifer out in the car, they went for a ride to the coast. It took a while but he felt he needed to keep practising even though he was now official. They got to the beach as a lot of families were going home. Tim had a picnic that his mum had made; a few sandwiches, crisps, quiche and strawberries, plus a cold flask with blackcurrant juice. They looked out to the horizon and they could see children still in the sea, adults walking dogs and boats bobbing up and down.

"Wow," said Tim, "it's like we are on holiday again, this is the life." Jennifer picked up a strawberry, "We could do this a lot now I can drive. Do you fancy camping next weekend? I can see if they have any reservations near here. I saw a campsite a mile down the road. Let's ask on the way back."

The picnic was just right and they both walked back the car. Tim got his camera out, "I'll take your photo, Jennifer. I want the sea in the background plus you learning against the car." Just as Tim was about to press the button a passer-by said he would take a picture of them both.

"Perfect," replied Tim, "Thank you so much." The couple drove up the road and pulled over at the campsite. Tim paid a deposit for two people in a 1x2-man tent. They were booked for next Friday until Sunday. Tim drove the car home. He had never driven in the dark, he was not ready for it yet so he wanted to get back soon.

Tim started going through the garage the day before their trip, he wanted to make sure he had everything they needed for the camping trip. He made a checklist: tent and pegs, hammer, a big blow up mattress with a fitted sheet, two pillows, quilt, foot pump, saucepans, frying pan, cooker, gas bottle, cutlery, plates, cups, mugs, kettle, water bottle, sharp knife, disposable BBQ, cans of coke, juice, coffee, tea, powdered milk, water bottle, plus a small box of food, not forgetting a wash bag and clothes. He hoped he hadn't forgotten anything. He drove to Jennifer's; she was ready at the door with her bag and she looked radiant. Bob and Julia waved goodbye.

"Please ring us when you arrive so we can relax," said Julia, "and have the best time this weekend."

The drive to the campsite was busy. "Other people must have the same idea," said Jennifer.

"No rush," replied Tim, "we have all day."

The vibe was good between them,. Tim turned the radio on and Jennifer relaxed back into the chair, put on her sunglasses and sang along to the tunes.

At the campsite, they both checked in, they were shown the spot to pitch their tent by a grumpy member of staff.

"Probably annoyed because she was in the middle of her cuppa," said Tim laughing.

The tent was easy to put up as it was a pop up one, the inner lining was more confusing and the toggles were put in the wrong place the first time, inside the tent it was hot.

"Let's keep the door open and keep the area cool," said Jennifer. Tim set the cooking stuff and other bits in the porch area. They had forgotten to bring chairs so Jennifer suggested sitting on the rug and cushions from the car. They then sat down, "Yes we've done it," said Tim. Suddenly they heard raised voices. It was their camping neighbours arguing. It turned out they had taken the tent on holiday but not the rods. They had driven for six hours and they were fuming. They got back in their car to go to the nearest camping shop to get a new tent. Tim opened a bottle of wine and poured them both a cup. The sun was out, the campsite was big, it had a pool at the end near the gate, a clubhouse, camper van area plus the tent field where they had been placed.

Next thing the neighbours were back erecting a new tent. Tim asked if they wanted a hand.

"Yes please," was the reply.

"We bought the first one we could see in the shop; its massive and I have no idea where to start, it was colour coded for the rods."

Tim read the instructions and the tent was up ten mins later. Tim went back to Jennifer. "Look, they gave me a four pack of cider for helping. That is nice," he said.

That night they made sausages and onions with rolls, had a can of cider each and chatted to the neighbours. *What a great first day,* Tim thought to himself.

On the second day, they woke up early and they could hear birds singing everywhere. Tim opened the tent and threw bread by the door. He set his camera up on the tripod, he did not wait long and snapped five birds all fighting over his crust of bread. Jennifer slept while Tim then read his book and had a coffee and then went for a walk. He got back and Jennifer was wide awake, showered and dressed. She had cereal. Looking outside, she saw children were playing bat and ball, also riding bikes on the campsite, and the grass was immaculate. The clubhouse had a quiz and disco on that evening which they had agreed to go to; today would be spend on the beach.

Jennifer had caught the sun as she had forgotten her sunscreen. They walked back to the tent and waved to the neighbours. Jennifer found her hat and sat in the shade. They were having burgers for dinner with salad, Tim lit the disposable BBQ after placing it on bricks and placed the patties on the rack. The smell was making them extra hungry; they had snacked earlier at the beach on ham rolls from the kiosk and ice cream. Jennifer chopped up tomato, cucumber and lettuce, dinner was served.

Later, they checked the time. "Let's get ready for the quiz," said Tim. They got ready in shorts and shirts, zipped the tent and went to the bar. They both had a beer, sat down and were chatting about the car and how they should give it a name when the neighbours joined the table.

"Do you mind if we join you? No other seats are available," said Tony.

"Of course," said Tim, "are you here for the pop quiz?"

"Yes," said Tony, "don't tell anyone but I'm a DJ. Did I mention Tina and I got married last year? The love of my life." They both laughed. They had a good night but did not win the quiz, and neither did Tony and Tina.

After a few rounds of drinks, the hall turned into a disco; no one noticed the chairs being moved to create a dance floor. The music was 70s style and the dancing was hilarious. It could have been a dad dancing competition; even the two TTs from the next tent were rubbish on the dance floor; in fact, Tony looked drunk.

Tina came over to ask Tim if he could help get Tony back to the tent. It was 11pm, she could not do it on her own. Outside the bar Tim found a shopping trolley, they got Tony in and wheeled home back to the tent field. Tony was dragged out of the trolley then into his bed; job done. What a funny night! They were in hysterics about it. Sunday, was check out day. Jennifer started packing everything up; the bed, mattress and inner tent. The rest could be put away after breakfast. Tim had bought croissants and jam; it was perfect with a cup of tea. They could hear Tony and Tina snoring; the walls were thin. They packed the car and left, stopping at a beach shop to buy humbugs and rock, then drove home.

A few weeks later, Tim contacted an agency to help track down his real parents. He answered each of the questions, as he had all the information needed from his Mum, Mary, and Dad, David. Tim had promised they would both always be his number one in his life, and he truly meant it.

A few days later, Tim received a letter to say they had found the information he had wanted about his biological parents, and it was not good news; both had been involved in a major car accident a few years earlier and they were killed instantly. Tim was devasted to hear this shocking news; it was a major blow to him, it took the wind out of his sails. He had been genuinely excited about the search. The letter went on to state that he did have siblings who were older and were happy to meet up.

His siblings were Paul Johnson, 26, and Sally Johnson, 28. Tim wasted no time at all in writing to them at the address he was given.

The thought of finally having extended family from the past thrilled him no end; he could not stop smiling, it was the icing on the cake.

Sometime after, a meeting took place between Tim, Paul and Sally.

Tim will never forget the day he met his siblings; it is etched in his memory. He remembers how nervous he had been when going to bed the night before, changing his mind about the clothes he would wear, what shoes would look best with his trousers and whether to wear his black smart jacket or camel casual one. The alarm went off and he ate a small amount of toast and had half a cup of tea then showered quickly wondering how the day would go. Before leaving home his dad sat him down on the sofa. Tim looked at his dad and said, "Dad, I'm so nervous. This is a big event and all I'm is what if they won't like me."

"Of course, they will like you, Tim. Why wouldn't they?"

Tim looked down at the floor and said, "Ohh, my mind is in overdrive, what if I start stammering? I am so nervous about this meet up."

His dad put his hand on his son's leg, looked him in the eye and said, "Tim, there is nothing not to like. Be brave and enjoy your journey and please tell us about it when you get home."

At this point his mum walked in the door and sat next to Tim. She gave him a hug, then a kiss on the cheek saying, "See you later Tim, we both love you, never forget that."

The venue for the meeting was a small drive away in a country pub called The King's Head. The pub opened at 10:30. As Tim got out of his vehicle, he noticed two people walking towards him. They were both smiling and shouting hello and straightaway Tim felt calm. His siblings were so welcoming; he noticed they all looked alike.

His brother was a bit taller and his sister a little shorter. They all hugged each other and laughed nervously Paul took the lead and said, "Oh, what a fantastic day this is. We are both so happy to meet you at last. We have been hoping for this day but never thought it would happen."

Tim took the handkerchief out of his pocket and blew his nose, he felt overwhelmed.

Sally then looped her arm in Tim's, looked at him and said, "You are not leaving us again. You are our blood. We want to know everything about you. Did you bring your photo album?"

"Yes," said Tim, "let's get a drink and get out table."

With that they all walked into the pub. Sally ordered tea and fruit cake, they all sat down at the table that had been reserved.

Paul was telling Tim how they had known about him all their lives, how thrilled the family were that he had got in touch, and how it was a day they had been waiting for.

Tim could see by his brother's eyes that he meant every word, his first impression of Paul was how genuine and well-spoken he came across; he had an aura about him and smart too in a nice pair of chinos with matching jumper. He also wore trendy glasses. He was a manager for an import export company and worked long shifts he earned good money. Sally had long blonde hair, no make-up but lots of jewellery. She had two rings on both hands, a big gold chain necklace and big earrings. She had a long brown dress on and brown leather boots. She was clutching her handbag to her body as if it would run away any minute which made Tim laugh to himself.

Sally was very warm in personality, very relaxed. She came across as a lovely lady; she worked as a nurse a few times a week in the evenings. She would start at 7:30 pm and finish at 8 am. It was tiring but she loved it and found it rewarding.

Sally wanted to know everything she was buzzing with excitement.

Before anything, Tim wanted to see photos of his biological parents, he wanted to know everything; when they were born, where they had lived, how they had met. It was the start of his journey.

The meeting went on for four hours. Tim had shared his photos of his childhood and upbringing along with his parents and grandparents on both sides. He was also taking home a small shoebox of pictures from his biological family; he had everything he needed in his hands.

With photographs shared and a promise to stay in touch regularly, they parted. Paul and Sally both were married and had children; Paul had two boys, and Sally three girls – Tim was over the moon with all this news. He was part of something. Plus, the good news was that they did not live too far either – only an hour's drive away.

Tim found out from his siblings a bit more about his real Mum and Dad.

His mum was called Katie and she was a singer.

His dad was called Andrew and he worked in the theatre industry, writing scripts for musicals.

It all now made sense, this was completely different to the lifestyle in which he had grown up.

Katie and Andrew decided on having just two children due to work commitments and lifestyle. So, when Katie realised that she was pregnant with a third, she was shocked; she could not cope, and that is when they decided to give the baby up for adoption – to help a couple who wanted a child but could not. It was all arranged, that was what happened.

Tim went on many trips with his brother and sister, Jennifer would go along too sometimes. It could be days out to the beach, walks in the sand dunes, collecting shells, and having a picnic; he would paddle in the sea with his nieces and nephews, play bat and ball – he was a different person when with his little family gang. He sometimes wondered what it would have been like to not have been adopted and to have stayed in the family – he loved having his siblings around.

Writing had always been Tim's passion; he would get letters in the post and phone calls from his siblings about things they had been doing, he was always dreaming and getting ideas of what he wanted to do in the future.

He also enjoyed spending time with his nieces and nephews, he had changed his behaviour and was now being sociable and spending more time with others – something he had only been able to do with his close family. Tim had got to the age of a young adult and the only real friend he had was

Jennifer; he knew it was out of his comfort zone but wanted to break this bad habit.

A few days later Tim and Jennifer drove the graveyard where his biological parents were buried, he laid a wreath next to the black headstone with gold lettering reading, "Paul Johnson and Kate Johnson sadly taken, together forever." Tim said a prayer, took a photo and left. He was quiet on the journey home; it was the closest he would ever get to his parents.

When Tim was 20, his grandmother Nanna Smith passed after a short illness of lung cancer – she was so poorly and did not have long to live. The doctor suggested that she go to the hospice for her final days. Imagine when Tim went to visit his beloved Nanna; he was to see his Bengal drawing in the room which was one of the winning pictures in the school competition all those years ago. It was hanging opposite the hospital bed. He felt closer to his Nanna than ever. He held her frail hand as she drifted in and out of consciousness, until her breathing got shallow, she passed away peacefully in her sleep. It was devastating, as Tim had never known anyone in his real life who had passed away.

His grandfather's heart was broken, he found it hard to continue the farm without his loving wife to sit with in the evening and chat with.

Nanna's funeral took place in a little chapel in the cemetery. Jennifer held Tim's hand through the service and helped him through all the tears he cried, all the time he was touching his silver bracelet that she had given him all those years earlier.

David and Mary suggested that Grandad move in with them permanently to sell the farm and the land – they would build a wooden lodge in the garden, he could be as sociable or unsociable as he wanted to be.

So, over the coming months the lodge was built, and Grandad Smith seemed happy again. Tim was a regular visitor with Jennifer.

Tim also at this time inherited a chunk of money from his Grandad.

With the help of his father, Tim bought a big piece of land with a barn in situ; Tim wanted to use this area to help local children learn how to grow food.

Tim wasted no time in planting apple, pear and cherry trees and then a section for his grape vines.

The rest, he sectioned into areas for crops, potatoes, carrots, parsnips, turnips, swede and onions.

He spoke with the local principal of the junior school and arranged gardening lessons with the children helping him – they would have an area to grow green beans, tomatoes, garlic, beetroot and lettuce which they would be able to take home.

They also planted blackberries, blackcurrant and raspberry bushes.

The barn was being converted into a crèche and toddler group, with staff by day, and after school club for afternoon and school holidays – creating jobs in the area. In the evening it was also to become a community centre.

The creche took longer to get up and running. The room to be used had a small kitchen area with little garden to the side; this was fenced off with lots of outdoor toys. Everything had to be inspected and passed, the creche was registered and the staff working there had to have certificates in childcare, diplomas and NVQs, including first aid and food hygiene. The staff were police-checked too; it was a safe space, with a locked door in and out.

Jennifer ran the administration for the child group – they had books and toys donated from local shops, special flooring from the local specialists in the town, a kitchen donated by a superstore and many other donations including small tables and chairs, rugs, games, paints, pads, black board, chalks of every colour of the rainbow, bookcases and books.

It was soon full every day of the working week; the creche was open 7 am until 6 pm (all except bank holidays).

The gardening lessons would be with a schoolteacher, with ten children on Monday, Wednesday, and Friday in the afternoons at 1 pm for 90 mins.

The allotment took a while to set up too as the ground was rock hard. A man had seen a small advent in the local paper and offered to rotovate the ground for free – the areas were sectioned ready for the children's plots and the adults too.

One area was sprinkled with wildflowers, creating a lovely border to split to plots up; it would look fantastic when summer arrived.

The adult plots were around 250 square metres, it was on a first come first served basis. The plots were gone within 90 mins of being advertised, ten in all. The owners could put up a small shed, but no fences; the outside was fenced off with a gate and padlock, each member had a key to the lock and access to the water. The annual charge was £90.

The plot holders would even do a swap shop in the allotment store area, swapping seeds and vegetable plants.

The barn was renamed The Meeting Place.

Jennifer offered to help with the bookings – she and Tim were now very much an item, and very much in love.

A music licence was given to The Meeting Place and the activities were able to be arranged and booked thanks to Jennifer.

Monday; Ballet and Tap with Linda. Beginners: 6–7. Intermediate: 7–8.

Tuesday; Ballroom Dancing with Roberta: 7–9

Wednesday; Pilates and Yoga with Michelle. Pilates: 7–8. Yoga 8–9.

Thursday; Snooker and Darts: 7–10.

Friday; Family night. 1st Friday of every month. Disco: 7–11.

Saturday; Birthdays, Weddings, etc. 7–12

The list was as follows:

Monday was ballet and tap dancing; the young girls would love to dress in a tutu and leotard and tie their hair in a bun and practice, practise, practice.

Tuesday, the ballroom dancing was for all ages; the dancing was fun, and you got to dance with everyone in the room.

Wednesday was Pilates and yoga; the instructor would get the group relaxed and in all kinds of positions.

Thursday, darts, and snooker – every Thursday, the teams would play another team in the community. The Meeting Place would supply sandwiches for all the players.

Every Friday at the beginning of the month there would be a disco for the community to all attend as wished; you did not have to be a member. The discos always went down a storm, the DJ would play all kinds of music and encourage the audience with competitions for the best dancing and karaoke; it was a big hit every month. Also, a raffle would take place with prizes of vouchers and gifts.

Saturdays, the hall was left for any bookings for parties, birthdays, anniversaries and weddings. Life was good but one thing was missing (a wife).

On one of the family nights, Tim was at the bar chatting to Jennifer when he felt a tap on his shoulder. He turned around and was face to face with the bully from school whose nose Tim had made bleed.

The bully, Jon, shook Tim's hand and could not apologise enough for his behaviour back in the school days. He said "sorry" a few times and blamed his behaviour on the way his dad had bought him up; his dad had been in and out of prison and the house had no rules, all the children were wild. Jon asked if he could join the darts team on Thursdays. Tim would never hold a grudge and he found it challenging work to not like someone so Jon joined the darts team and he was incredibly good, soon moving to captain. What a turnaround, from bully to bestie; you could not make it up!

When Tim is 23, he visited Mr and Mrs Jacobs at the farm. He let them both know that he would love to make Jennifer his wife – Mr & Mrs Jacobs were over the moon. Tim wasted no time explaining his feelings and love for their daughter and left the farm with a big smile on his face and their blessing.

Tim visited Jennifer at The Meeting Place – it was not open yet and Jennifer was tidying up the reception area. Tim stood in front of her and dropped down on one knee. Jennifer gasped as she had no idea that this was going to happen. With tears in her eyes, she replied with a massive "YES."

Tim could not stop smiling; his beautiful Jennifer was going to be his wife. They both wanted to be married quickly; they rang the registry office the next day – the wedding was booked for two weeks' time.

Jennifer's mum made her a dress; Tim's real brother would be best man and Tim's real sister would be a flower carrier. Grandad Jones made the wedding cake. Nanna Smith's wedding ring would be passed down as a heirloom and special present from Grandad Smith.

The Meeting Place would hold the reception, Tim's nieces and nephews plus the gardening kids sang as Jennifer walked into her wedding looking spectacular. Jennifer looked like she was going to burst as she walked in. The dress was cream and off the shoulder, tight on the bodice, flared out at the hips and knee length, the veil was to the shoulders. Jennifer's hair had been softly washed and curled. She looked like a film star; she wore ivory heels. Tim held his breath as she walked towards him as he had never seen her look so pretty. He was proud of her and looking forward to her being his wife. Jennifer looked at her husband-to-be; he was wearing black shoes and tie, a white shirt and navy-blue suit, had a flower pinned to it plus handkerchief in the pocket.

"Wow," said Jennifer, "you scrub up good."

Tim smiled and replied, "I was about to say the exact same thing."

The wedding commenced. Tim glanced over to his mum, she had tears in her eyes, tears of happiness. The after-wedding party was to be a hog roast and the tables had red and white wine in jugs, gold napkins, gold candles, white flowers, gold balloons with white tablecloths plus gold sprinklings dusted over giving the finishing look. The guests sat down while Tim and Jennifer and both sets of parents had the top table. The speeches came and went. Tim spoke about his new wife and how he felt grateful to have a special lady as his partner and wife. She brushed away a tear. He then presented her with the biggest bouquet she had ever seen. Lots of photos were taken during the day, afternoon and evening, the dancefloor was cleared, the DJ played all the party songs he had and more. The wedding went without a hitch and everyone had a fantastic day. It was attended by all the friends who used The Meeting Place; local staff from the farms, the school staff, plus members of the groups who use the venue, including the darts and snooker team. It was a dream day the best of his life so far.

Tim would start writing his life books about how to live it and enjoy it.

Tim was still reading a lot of books, he learnt much about many different subjects.

He authored short books about bullying, stammering and adoption to start with, then longer books about losing a grandparent, being an only child and farm life. His books were selling well too, and making money for him. He was an author which was the last item on his tick list.

Tim and Jennifer bought a three-bedroom cottage with a small garden and fantastic views. Tim felt like the richest man in the world; he had a lovely family, a lot of friends and a beautiful wife. It was equivalent to winning the lottery.

Nine months after the wedding, Jennifer gave birth to a baby boy weighing eight lbs; the baby was named David Tim (DT for short). A year later, followed by twins Isabella and Lucy.

Four years passed and Tim is still pinching himself about his lucky life. He reflects on his past, lonely, bullied life and his stammer; his loving, caring upbringing by his adopted parents, Mary and David, and was so grateful for his life. The skills he was taught by his dad, the time and love from both grandparents and lastly meeting Jennifer and falling in love. You cannot buy this happiness. He thought back to what he has accomplished with The Meeting Place, the happy faces everyday by all the people who used the venue and the smiles on the school children's faces as they leave the site with bags of potatoes and onions.

On 24th December 2023, an appointment was booked at Tattoo Ink. Tim walked in and showed a sketch he had drawn of two designs that he wanted interlinked; he wanted to show his love to Mary and David, and both his grandparents.

The tattooist got to work – two hearts were inked on his upper left arm with Mum and Dad, Nanna and Grandad intertwined; it looked special. Tim had tears in his eyes when he saw the finished inking; a perfect tribute to the six adults who had always been there for him.

Tim walked into his home after an early morning stroll; it was Dec 25th, 2023, and his 30th birthday.

Everyone he loves is in the room, ready to raise a birthday toast to him. As he walked around, shaking hands, he pinched himself and wondered if this was dream. *No, it is real life, and I am loving every minute.*

Life does not get any better than that.

THE END

PS. Jennifer's was celebrating her 30th birthday a few weeks later December 31st; Tim had bought her a new silver chain bracelet to match the old one she had given him all those years ago.

Epilogue

Tim would visit his parents every Sunday with Jennifer and the family. His grandparents always turned up too to see the children and they would play in the garden as they did with Tim all those years ago. Afterwards the they would walk over the Jacobs' Farm for a roast dinner; Jake and Emma had moved into the farm, they would carry on the ritual of the afternoon walk. It took longer these days. Bob had a puppy, a Jack Russell called Jessie and she kept everyone entertained. Life was perfection with a capital P.

A Poem for My Wife

I raise a glass to my lovely life,
I'm grateful to Jennifer for being my wife,
I burst with joy when looking around,
Up high to the sky and low to the ground.

My children I will never love more,
It's all you need as I used to be poor,
You do not need anything but love,
It is like putting your hand in a glove.

I met you and our love grew,
I'd walk a hundred miles to be with you,

I love you Jennifer, thank you for always supporting my dreams. Xx.